Taste

The author and the artist

Dustin Warburton is an award-winning international children's author, screenwriter, and horror writer. He's best known for writing the stories for such films as Spiders 3D, Black Asylum, and the most publicized children's book in the world in 2012/2013, "Dennis the Wild Bull." With over 14 books published his work has been featured on The Tonight Show, Late night with Jimmy Fallon, Oprah, Time Magazine, Sports illustrated and many others.

Nathan Gorman grew up in the same rural community. His family owns the General Store in the town. Nathan's artistic abilities were evident at an early age, as he often cut up newspapers and magazines to create portraits. Or he made stone chairs out of the crumbling rock walls behind his parents' farmhouse. After attending art school in Pittsburgh, Nathan moved back to N.Y. and has worked as a chef in Ithaca for many years.

When Nathan and Dustin first met in 1996, they knew they were going to work together on a book. It took over ten years for their paths to cross and the story to emerge. This book is a horror story about the town they both grew up in.

Taste

Written By Dustin Warburton

Illustrated By Nathan Gorman

Cover By Stephen Blickenstaff

Copyright© 2006
Dustin Warburton and Nathan Gorman

All rights reserved. No part of this book may be reproduced in any form, except for the inclusion of brief quotations in a review, without permission in writing from the author or publisher.

Library of Congress Control Number 2024920300

ISBN 978-1-7372057-5-3

First published in 2006.

I want to thank my wife, family and friends
- Nathan Gorman

I want to thank everyone that has
supported me over the years. It's been quite the journey.
-Dustin Warburton

Table of Contents

The author and the artist 2

Prologue ix

Chapter 1 1

Chapter 2 15

Chapter 3 25

Chapter 4 30

Chapter 5 49

Chapter 6 62

Prologue

Fear.......? It is an overwhelming force we all experience at one time or another. The specters surprise their victims when they least expect it. Every man contains his own inner demon, a demon constructed from the absolute horrors of the mind. If a certain individual gives in to these hidden desires, these elements of destruction, he is forever diminished, losing his soul in the process of transmigration.

This is when a higher form of life exceeds your own.

They might visit you in your dreams, while your mind is traveling through its own world of creativity, where reality comes to an abrupt halt, and your imagination becomes the key to fulfillment. In the beginning, the victim's inner strength will rise to the surface, bringing about a stronger, more determined state of mind. After this occurs, the unholy presence sweeps its victim with the intriguing gift of "Hope." And then, when the victim's hopes are at their extreme fullest, it will come crashing down as the walls of reality crumble in front of their very own eyes. You can't even estimate what pure and devious evil is capable of doing. If you ever think, just for a moment, that you might stand a chance in beating the forces of evil, which are regarded as "fairy tales" you are letting yourself be fooled, since you don't stand a chance in the mere depths of oblivion. They'll find you whenever they feel the need to do so, no matter where you are, even if you're fast asleep in your own bed after a late night movie. They just wait very patiently, for the right time. Time is but a mere clock. Their patience has learned to expand through countless lifetimes, making them unstoppable.

So don't bother praying. It won't help you. Don't bother pleading. It can't save you. There is absolutely nothing you can do to prevent the inevitable. You must also remember one thing. Remember the past as if it were tomorrow, and only then will you learn what your fate shall be.

Published in 1999, New England Young Writers Conference Anthology

Chapter 1

After the Revolutionary war, New York State added additional counties in order to establish residence within its lands. Frontiersman as well as former soldiers hiked into the uncut forest that covered most of the state. Uninhabited land was an opportunity for the taking.

In 1796 a group of seven frontiersmen (four of whom were former soldiers) traveled through the Catskills and headed for the most untouched area left in the state, Chenango County. It was the geographical center of the state. The Onondaga Indians had recently given the land up. A deadly plague swept through the Indian tribes, wiping them out one by one. The land they once occupied went unclaimed.

Once the men reached Chenango County they traveled along the Chenango River. The river's shore had a reputation for famine and disease, along with frequent Indian raids. The only known settlements in the county were along the river. The men planned to examine each town with a keen eye and determine the next phase of their journey by what they had learned as they passed through the towns. It wasn't long after they started down the river that three of the men suddenly became ill and died within days.

- Taste -

- Taste -

The three bodies were thrown overboard into the murky water below.

The remaining four men were former soldiers, and their instincts were to get as far away from the area as soon as possible. They ditched their boat near a village called Oxford, and then headed west into uncharted territory. The land was untamed and overgrown. The only visible evidence of human habitation was the scattered Indian trails the men would come across from time to time.

The group's leader was a man named Sylvanus Moore. The three men who traveled alongside him were his younger brothers, Ike, Jeremiah, and Jesse. All three admired Sylvanus for his vast wisdom and leadership skills. After the war Sylvanus and his three brothers stayed close together as they made the transition from military life to frontiersmen.

The men had traveled thirty-seven miles from Oxford when they came upon a clearing at the bottom of a valley. A stream ran alongside, leading the men to a lake slightly above, nestled in the rocky soil. Surrounded by jagged cliffs and deep gorges, this unique place provided isolation as well as rich farmland. Their journey was over and the work began.

They cleared wilderness to make suitable farm land. They dammed streams to power the mills they were building. Houses and churches sprang up. Prosperity was evident in this settlement, which now was called Moore.

By 1811 the settlement had transformed into a bustling hamlet. The lake, now called the Genegantslet, powered two tanneries, a foundry, a grist mill and a woolen mill. Two stores faced each other on the main intersection of the hamlet. One of the stores sold animal feed and farming supplies, and the other one catered to the townspeople's needs. Both stores were owned by Sylvanus and his brothers. Across the street from the stores were two vacant lots, also owned by the soldiers. With the new settlers

- Taste -

- Taste -

building their houses steadily farther from the center of town, this corner land became very desirable.

In the summer of 1812 a man entered the town by stagecoach in the early evening. Dressed entirely in black clothing and wearing a top hat, he entered one of the stores asked to speak to the owner. Sylvanus came out of the back and greeted this odd-looking man. The stranger was very tall and extremely skinny. He resembled a scarecrow the way his shoulders shrugged as he stood or walked.

"I believe this settlement is in need of a postmaster" the man said as he blew his nose in to a blue handkerchief.

Sylvanus stood still as he regarded the stranger's gestures and analyzed this first encounter. Sylvanus looked at him for a moment and then said,

"Yes, yes of course we do," he laughed out loud and smacked the stranger on his back. "Why, I think that's the one thing this town needs. We've got everything else. In fact we need this," Sylvanus reached his hand out and gave a firm shake.

"What is your name, sir?" he asked while he continued to shake hands. The stranger removed his hand and blew his nose once more. He then puffed out his chest and stood tall, trying to straighten his corked body.

"John Hill," he smiled with delight.

It wasn't long after this encounter that John Hill had acquired both vacant lots across from the stores. Hill's father had been a wealthy merchant, so money wasn't an issue. Now he owned half of the intersection and already had workers building in both lots. Across from the general store was a massive three-story building which was going to stand as a hotel and post office. Across from the feed store in the more wooded lot was going to be John Hill's home. The architectural design was that of a southern plantation house. Massive pillars extending from top to bottom bordered the front porch of the mansion. Windows were placed in different patterns along each side of the home. A diamond shaped window was placed high above the front porch, directly below the hip roof which angled down as though it were a pyramid. The overall effect of this window was to give the impression the house had an eye.

Looking out at all who walk past.

Both buildings were finished within two years. During that time John Hill had already established a post office inside his own wooden shack where he'd been living during the construction of his home and hotel. He also fell in love with a beautiful young woman named Elizabeth Turner. The hard work was over and now it was a time for celebration. Hill moved his post office in to the three- story building that now stood as a hotel for traveling pioneers as well as a post office for the townspeople. He then moved his new wife and baby into the mansion. Long had he dreamed of this structure being built and finally his vision was complete. Standing tall and as powerful as the churches nearby, the mansion was known as the Hill House.

Sylvanus Moore and his three brothers still held a tight grasp on the farming aspect of this hamlet. Each lived on a separate farm and sold their products in the stores they owned. Hill, on the other hand, was the town's first postmaster and had established along with the post office a very profitable hotel. The location of this hamlet was at the crossroads of the Adirondacks and Catskill Mountains, making it a significant intersection. Many distant travelers made their way through this hamlet for that reason alone. The population was now over 200 people and covered some fifty thousand acres.

- Taste -

- Taste -

The year was now 1815. Nineteen years had passed since Sylvanus Moore and his brothers first settled in the area. John Hill had been living in the hamlet for only three years and had made quite a name for himself in the process. Everything seemed to be going as well as it possibly could have, until the morning of October 14, 1815.

When both stores didn't open as they routinely did, it raised many questions in the town. After a few hours passed and there still wasn't any sign of Sylvanus or his brothers, a few of the local tradesmen and farmers traveled out to Sylvanus's farm outside of town. Sylvanus could not be found. There was no sign of him anywhere. After searching his land and coming up with nothing, the men quickly traveled to one of the other soldier's homes. There too, they found nothing. Untouched food remained cold on plates.

They moved on to the next soldier's home, where it was the same. They found nothing and discovered no one. This action repeated once more and the group suddenly found themselves in a serious situation. Sylvanus Moore and his three brothers were missing.

Meanwhile a father and son who were hunting a mile or so behind the Hill estate came upon a grisly site. They had shot a deer and were tracking the scattered drops of blood when they found what appeared to be the remains of a human body. The head was severed from the carcass and laid some twenty feet away from the slab of flesh that used to resemble a torso. The arms and legs were ripped away and were scattered about in a grotesque manner. It appeared as if something had totally dismembered the body. The father, whose name was Tom Swanson, knelt down beside the head and rolled it over in order to see its face. He suddenly stepped back in terror and grabbed his son and ran back to town to fetch help.

- Taste -

The face was that of John Hill.

A hunting party was formed to retrieve the body. When the party reached the spot where the body had been they discovered it was gone. Blood-soaked earth remained, along with something else. Something Tom Swanson didn't see before. Unusual tracks were all over the blood stained area. Each set of tracks ran into one another, making it appear that whatever made the tracks simply disappeared in thin air. These men were hunters and pioneers, but never before had any of them seen tracks such as the ones that covered this unholy spot. The tracks were never identified. As the men prepared to return to town they discovered a black top hat, soaked red. The hat was a very recognizable one indeed. It was that of John Hill. This they knew, but what they didn't know was what had happened to the man.

That evening the town was in a chaotic frenzy. The men found themselves in the hotel bar discussing what was to be done. Hill's wife had claimed he hadn't come home the night before. This was quite common since Hill worked in the hotel in the evenings. As to

Sylvanus and his brothers, there was nothing at all. Only Ike and Jesse had families and not even their families had been at home. Something very unusual was happening. It was as if the men had disappeared without a trace. And the only things that gave any clue at all to what was happening were the unidentified tracks and the top hat they had discovered

The father and son who originally found the body were questioned all through the night. They were not allowed to leave due to the paranoia which now swept over the town. Hill's wife remained with her baby in their home across the street.

The next morning the head of John Hill was discovered on the church

- Taste -

steps, two houses away from the Hill House. The locals began to think something evil was at work. Two days later, on October 17th, Mrs. Hill hung herself in the upstairs closet of their home. Her baby was found in the basement wrapped up in blankets. It appeared that she had suffocated the baby prior to taking her own life. Sylvanus and his brothers were still nowhere to be found.

As the evening of October 18th came around, the people in town found themselves gathering in the hotel once again. Four days had now passed since the unexplained events. People were reacting to this bizarre situation in different ways. Women and children stayed close together all through the night, singing songs and holding each other tight. The men argued in the bar while they reloaded their guns over and over again. Then without warning it happened.

The liquor bottles on the shelves startled to rattle and shake. People ran outside and found themselves being sucked into a torrent of water which devastated the town. The dam had broken and let loose a wave of terrible force. The flooding wiped away all the mills along the river's edge and deposited huge boulders all through the hamlet. Houses and farms were destroyed. Many people lost their lives on the night of October 18th.

During the flood, the hotel somehow caught fire and was destroyed within hours. Flaming wooden beams floated in the water. Desperate hands from within the icy water grasped the burning beams in a last attempt for survival. The flesh from people's fingers melted instantly as their bodies sank in to the darkness below. As the raging waters began to recede and the sun started to emerge through clouds of smoldering wood, the hamlet resembled nothing more than a watery grave. As survivors made their way through the knee- high water, they discovered body after body lying in the muddy water. The survivors banded together and a pile of dead carcasses was stacked up directly in front of the Hill House. Then the remains of the Hill family were gathered. The bodies were carried out behind the Hill Estate into the woods, where they were buried.

The flood victims were disposed of separately. A stone wall was built around the remains of John Hill, his wife and baby. Superstition now played a role in this new development: the stone wall surrounding the Hill family was an attempt to keep their spirits at bay.

The remaining families packed up all of their belongings and left this wasteland behind them in search of a new life elsewhere. The hamlet remained abandoned for over fifty years until the late

1860s, when it was resettled and renamed. The town was renamed McDonough. The new settlers were unaware of this area's past.

The events that occurred during the month of October in 1815 were forgotten long ago. The townsfolk who experienced the situation fled in terror and left the awful memories of what had happened behind them as well. Time conceals the truth remarkably.

To this day the town of McDonough still exists. Taking a stroll through the main intersection is like being thrown back a century or more to when horses were the means of transportation. The original two stores remain. A vacant lot sits where the hotel used to stand. Most of the original houses that survived the flood still run up and down the streets, worn down through years of neglect. All of the mills are now gone, but their stone foundations can still be found hidden within the rocky soil.

The Hill house still remains, abandoned and unused. It over-looks the town which has seen so much, almost as if it were a marker of what once was. The paint has worn away and many of the windows have been broken.

- Taste -

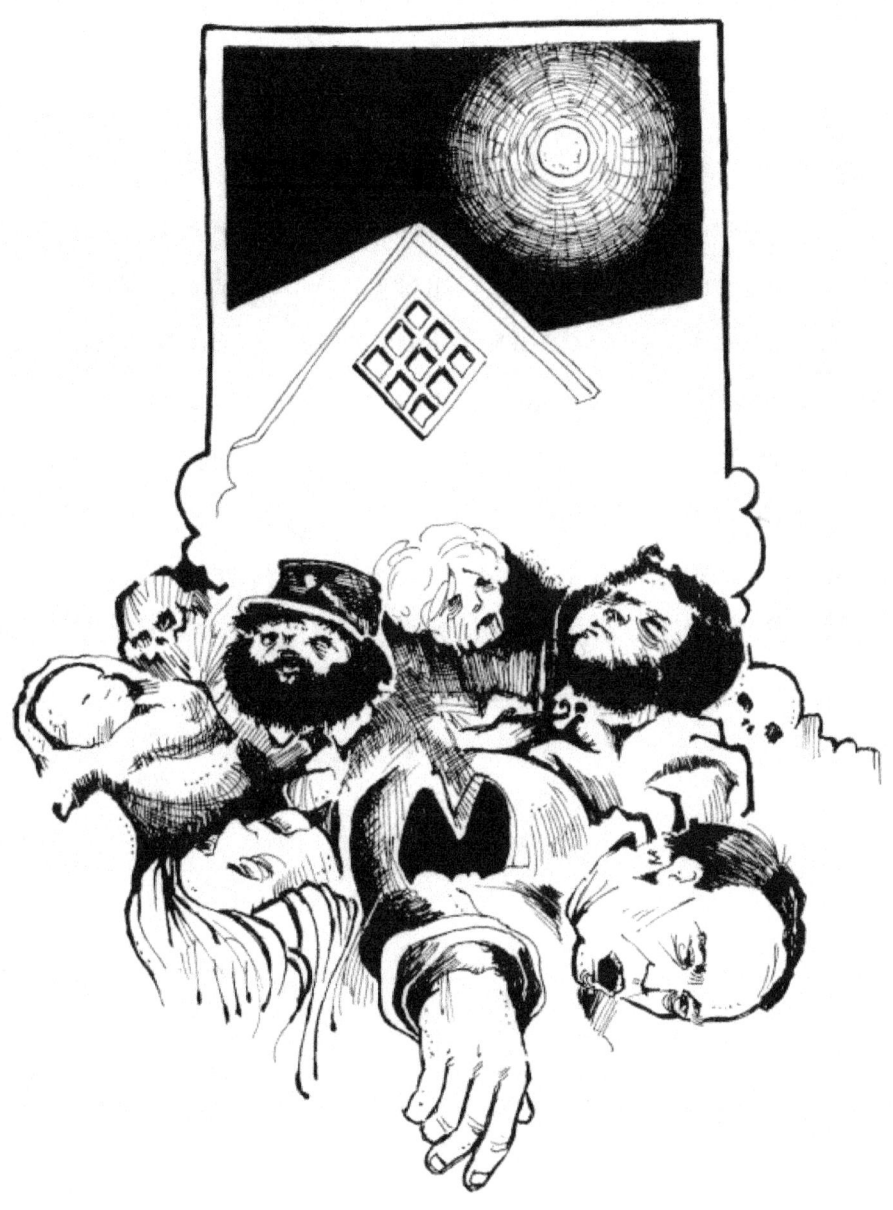

- Taste -

But one window still looks out to all who cross its path. The diamond-shaped window in the front is untouched and still attracts the attention of anyone who passes. People cannot resist the feeling that they are being watched as they look up towards the eye of the house.

Deep in the woods behind the house lie John Hill, his wife and daughter. Their graves remain covered in moss and hidden by the overgrown bushes and trees. All of the stories and secrets of many were forgotten, their epitaphs worn away from a century's weathering storms. No one remembers what happened in the settlement. As to the whereabouts of Sylvanus Moore and his brothers, answers were never found.

Somewhere out in the dark damp woods lies the answer. The bodies of the Hill family remain in the earth to this day, their souls watching every move we make, together as one. And somewhere out there the former soldiers watch from beneath the surface, waiting to show the world what it was they encountered so long ago.

Chapter 2

The weather was extremely chill this fine October day. October 14th it was. Late in the afternoon it appeared to be, 4:36 to be exact. A lone station wagon made its way up Dear Creek Path. For those of you who are not familiar with this stretch of pass, it's regarded as one of the worst seasonal roads in the southern tier of New York State. Isolated from the rest of the world, this place has found a way to stay dormant, unnoticed. Being totally surrounded by countless miles of state land can have that effect on the environment.

"A healthy batch for the master," a ghoulish voice said to itself as it glared toward the headlights, hiding behind the dark pines of old. Then it moved suddenly, springing its gruesomely limber body across the road.

"What was that!!!!!!!!!!!!?" The driver screamed in panic. The car swerved violently from side to side and was unable to stop due to its speed. The car immediately smashed into one of the deep muddy ditches that ran on both sides.

The unseen being paused as it snorted deeply, producing a gasping type sound. Inside the car were two panic-stricken teenagers who were unprepared for what they encountered this evening.

- Taste -

- Taste -

The passenger side tires of the car were completely engulfed in the muddy grave, which held their means of escape in a powerful grip.

The creature was viewing them from the back, hiding behind a large pine tree. As it breathed it sounded like an old man gasping for his last breath. Gurgling saliva dripped from its mouth.

"Did you see that?" the driver shouted as he wiped blood from his face. The sudden impact caused the driver's head to smash in to the rear view mirror, thus breaking his nose immediately and cracking the windshield where the mirror was attached.

"I didn't see anything but you wrecking your car, Tom," Nathan remarked angrily. Nathan looked down toward his chest and discovered he was covered in blood as well. His eyes lit up and his face was horrified.

"I mean look what the fuck's all over me, man." His hands were shaking and waving in the air, splattering blood all over the place as his fingers moved.

"I'm covered in your fucking blood, man. Look at me!" Tom's face was still, his eyes directly on Nathan's right shoulder. Tom's face suddenly grew pale and he remained silent.

Nathan shouted, "What the fuck are you looking at?" Nathan's eyes were now the size of half dollars.

Tom pointed to Nathan's shoulder and said,

"I don't think that's my blood, bro'," At that moment Nathan closed his mouth and sat back in the seat. His hands fell in to his lap. Sticking out of Nathan's shirt was a yellow and blue handle. Embedded in the flesh of his shoulder was the shaft of a screwdriver that must have been on the dash prior to the accident.

- Taste -

- Taste -

"Holy fuck, Tom, it's in me." The adrenaline was slowing down in his veins. The state of shock was wearing off. Reality had now come to the surface.

Tom rolled down his window and started to climb out.

"I've got to get to a hospital right now! Wait, where are you going?" Nathan cried out in pain. Tom rose to his feet and quicklyran to the rear of the car and opened the back hatch. Tom began to remove several wool blankets that concealed three large crates. "Tom," Nathan hollered out.

"I'd suggest you get yourself out of that car if you want to make it out of here before the sun goes down." Tom pulled out a 20 Gauge Ithaca deer slayer pump out of one of the crates.

Nathan realized what he had to do and frantically climbed out of his window.

As Nathan stood up he could hear Tom loading the gun.

"What are you doing?" Nathan said as he climbed through the muddy inferno.

Tom's face was rigid, his eyes wide. He had already loaded the gun within seconds of having it and was adjusting a belt which goes over the shoulder and connects at the waist. Ammunition was stored on the belt, enough to make a war of your own somewhere.

His movements were rapid and his speech appeared to be shaky.

"Whatever it was that jumped out in front of us is still out here, somewhere." He glared behind his back as he cocked the pump and prepared it for use.

Nathan was in a world of his own. He had lost a lot of blood and it was only a matter of time until fatigue set in and eventually loss of consciousness. He had to get to a hospital and he knew it. As far as the

- Taste -

thing in the woods, Nathan's mind wasn't on any of that. But Tom's mind was, for he had seen something he had never seen before. And for some sick reason, Tom knew it wouldn't be the last.

The hatch was shut and the doors were locked. Tom had his back pack on and quickly wrapped Nathan's shoulder with a rag he had made out of a shirt.

"Ready," Tom's voice was shaky from the shock of the entire event. The two of them started walking. They had been driving through the woods for at least half an hour; Tom knew they were miles from anything.

As the two staggering boys walked in a haze of confusion, eyes were watching them from the woods. It wasn't fifty feet away from the boys when it suddenly stopped and began to screech, creating an ungodly din for anyone who could hear its voice.

Tom and Nathan both jumped in panic and turned. The horrible noise was coming from near the car, of that they were certain. But what was it? Neither boy had ever heard anything like it before, and Tom was a hunter.

Nathan started to shake as he walked backwards; walking next to him was Tom with his gun pointed towards the car.

"What is it?" Nathan's voice struggled through sobs and tears. His eyes as well as his face appeared to be swelling. The red puffiness started to conceal his true image.

"I don't know, but I saw it," Tom said as he suddenly stopped. Nathan still moved. Tom had his eyes set on something, and now he began to move back towards the car, towards the horrible noise in the woods.

"What are you doing?" Nathan screamed. Instinct tells us to run from something fearful, at least that's what most people do. Nathan couldn't believe his eyes, at one point he actually rubbed them in order to wake himself up out of this nightmarish ordeal, but he wasn't sleeping. The events unfolding were real and Nathan had to come to terms with what was happening. He was seriously injured and deep in the forest, and he had lost a lot of blood already. Fear was setting in and Nathan was scared for his life. Then he thought about the noise coming from the woods and the thing that caused their accident. Although he didn't see it, he started to believe as he listened to the horrible noise coming from the forest, not far from where they stood. Panic was taking over his mind, combined with the loss of blood. Nathan did the only thing he had left, he began to run.

Tom didn't even look in Nathan's direction; his attention was on something else. As Nathan ran farther and farther away, Tom continued to walk toward his car. Within minutes Nathan was out of sight and Tom was only ten feet from the car. The noise had stopped for a few moments and so did Tom. He stood still and gripped his gun tight. His hands were sweating as he repositioned his fingers. The blood coming from his nose dripped off his chin as if it were a faucet.

Tom waited for something to happen and listened for the unearthly howl once more. Then something even more unusual happened, the wind stopped. The leaves that were blowing violently stopped immediately. Everything that causes a sound ceased to make a noise for that one instant in which Tom stood shaking in the middle of the woods with his gun pointed toward a target he did not see.

At that moment Tom's eyes were searching all over the place, unaware that he was being watched from beneath as well. Just as Tom started to take another step he heard something behind him and quickly turned around with a terrified expression on his face.

- Taste -

"Bang," a single gun shot startled Nathan as his attempt to run turned into a limping race for freedom. Nathan stopped and looked back. He didn't know what was happening and was confused. The gunshot was not a good sign.

"I've got to get out of here," he whimpered to himself as he continued to stagger. The farther Nathan traveled the thicker the trail of blood became. It wouldn't be long now, the fresh scent of blood was in the air and his prowler was on its way.

It wouldn't be long now. Follow the bloodstained path and you shall see. Follow the blood soaked earth and you will be forever kept in insanity.

- Taste -

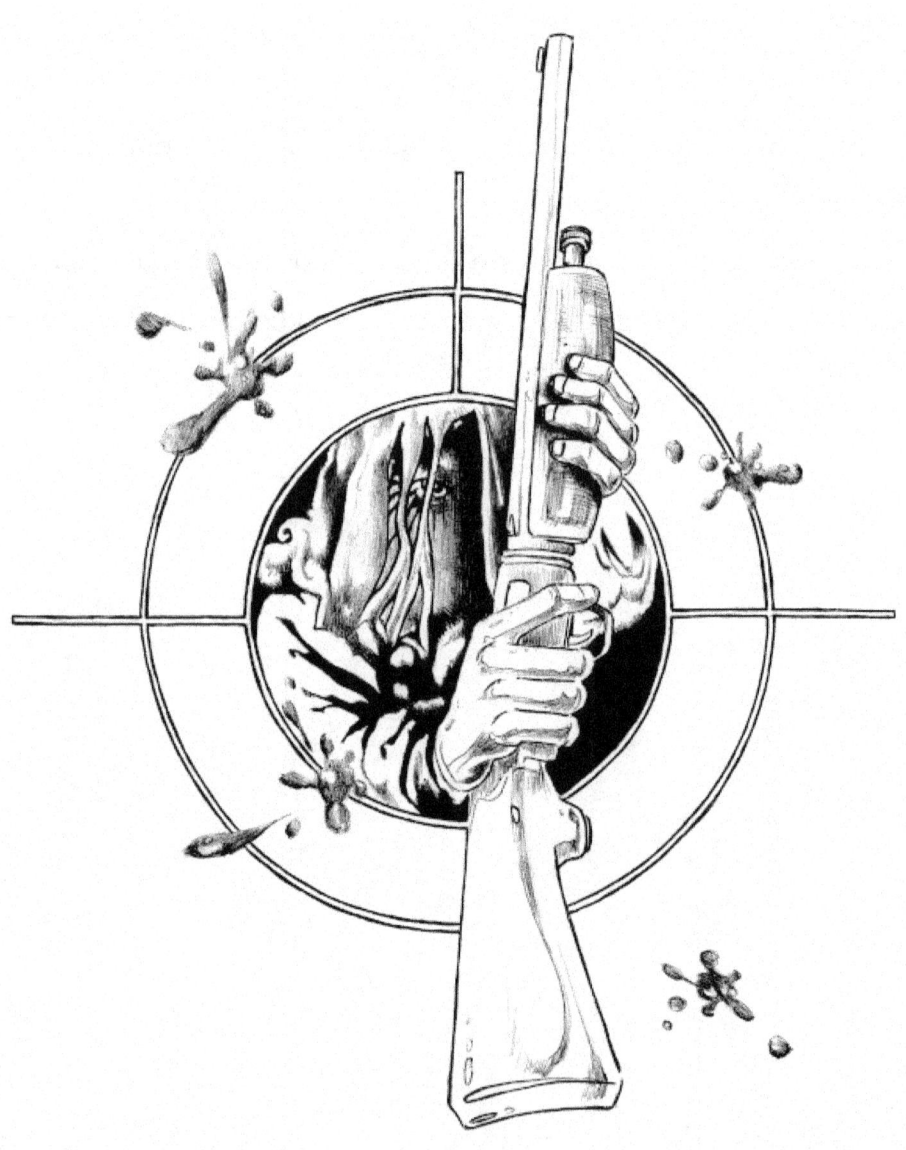

Chapter 3

Brandon McAllister was not like the other children. While the other neighborhood boys played tag football on the paved street outside, Brandon remained alone in his room, silent from the world. This was the room where he secretly opened the blinds with hopes of catching some sort of incident occurring. Maybe one of the boys would get hurt, scrape a knee. That type of thing was usually pleasant for Brandon. For Brandon was not like the other children.

His long dark hair was full of split ends. The thick glasses he wore made his eyes look like strobe lights. His skinny torso was covered with scars, most of them self-inflicted. The worst looking scar was 6 inches in length and located slightly below his right ear. This particular mark led to his name among the 9th grade society he grew to hate. They called him Gash and for that reason alone, he waged a silent war against the principles our society preached.

"Brandon," his mother shouted from the other room. Her voice startled him and he quickly jumped away from the window. He stood still for a moment and stared into his hands, then walked slowly in to the living room. His mother was extremely obese, weighing over 400 pounds.

- Taste -

- Taste -

Since moving around became more of a chore than a necessity, she hardly ever left her spot on the couch. The curtains were blocking any sunlight from seeping in and the lights were usually off. She always complained about the light. Brandon figured she'd just rather live in darkness in an attempt to isolate her self from the outside world. The stench in the living room was unbearable. Not moving much leads to not cleaning enough and this created an unfavorable aroma rising from her unwashed body. This particular odor, combined with the smell of 11 cats that lived alongside her produced an ammonia odor reaching as far as the yard outside their home.

"Brandon," she shouted again. "Where the hell are you?" Brandon was standing directly behind the couch – his hands were shaking.

"I'm right here, Mom," he whispered.

"Well, Jesus Christ, speak up boy; no wonder nobody wants anything to do with you. You don't even have the balls to talk like a man." As she spoke, her right arm waved in the air. Brandon stared at her arm, his eyes fixated on the elbow. Slowly her words became more distant and Brandon couldn't hear anything but a low pitched humming sound. Her arm still waved and her mouth still moved but nothing could be heard. Then the sound of a heartbeat emerged, slow but moving faster by the second.

Suddenly Brandon grabbed her right arm and sank his teeth deep into the elbow. Raging and biting, he bit down until he could feel his other hand on the opposite side. At that moment he pulled with all of his might and fell backwards on to the floor. With him he still had what was left of her arm lying in his lap. He quickly jumped to his feet and headed towards his bedroom. He threw her arm on the bedroom floor and placed his bloody hands over his ears. The heartbeat was getting louder. He backed up until he was against the wall. The arm was lying on the floor, surrounded by CD

- Taste -

covers and books. It was on top of a blue record case. The arm looked as though it belonged where it lay.

Brandon's face was tense, his mouth was open and lips were trembling. The screams of pain started to emerge slowly into his consciousness. He started hearing the howls coming from his bedridden mother. He looked around frantically, confused about what had happened. Brandon grabbed his head, closed his eyes and started screaming as loud as he could. Just then his eyes opened.

"Hey, you hear me?" Brandon shook his head from a daze-like experience and found himself standing behind a couch with his mother's hand waving in the air.

"What, Mom," he stuttered slowly.

"I said for the third time, go outside and grab the mail. What the hell's wrong with you, Brandon?" Brandon looked down toward his hands, they weren't shaking anymore.

"Yeah, Mom, I'll go get it."

As Brandon started walking out of the room his mom yelled out, "Let me know how it tastes." Brandon's head jerked back violently.

"How *what* tastes?" He snapped back in a paranoid tone.

"The Cajun chicken Mrs. Anderson brought back from the church dinner last night, let me know."

Brandon smiled to himself as he started walking again.

"Sure mom, I'll let you know how it tastes!"

Chapter 4

"Move it a little farther to the right; come on, put your shoulders into it!"

"Will you shut the hell up, Mike? I know what I'm doing." Jonathan Bush barked back at his friend as they both attempted to partake in somewhat of an illegal activity. The two troublemaking teens were in a cemetery directly behind the local church. Not far from the road, but very isolated as it was disguised by the overgrown wilderness. Here in the secluded world of our forgotten past these two young men are trying their luck at a new passion, grave robbing.

"On the count of four we'll both push, it's the only way," Jonathan said to Mike as he sweated from head to toe. Mike was sitting on top of another gravestone admiring their latest find.

Jonathan paused for a moment;

"You hear me?"

Mike looked up as he held a rusty watch in his hand.

"Hold on a second." Mike started looking over the watch once again. Jonathan was on his hands and knees near a stone crypt that he had been trying to open for the last hour and a half. This particular tomb had a stone

- Taste -

slab covering it which was eight feet long and four feet wide. It appeared that if the stone slab could be pushed to the side, it would reveal the coffin or whatever remains were underneath.

"Dude, we've got a lot of shit this time." Mike was looking through the bag they had filled throughout the day. Inside the bag were a few rings, pieces of metal, something that appeared to be the face of a watch. And a few other weird trinkets one would find in the soil of a graveyard.

"You know what we have to invest in, a metal detector." Mike said in a proud tone.

Suddenly the boys heard a loud cracking sound coming from near the church. The two of them were silent; both sets of eyes were widened by the idea of being caught. Mike jumped to his feet and threw the bag over his shoulder.

"What are you doing, do you see something?" Jonathan was now rising off the ground and getting ready to run.

"I know one thing, I'm sure as hell not getting caught," and with those words Mike was sprinting through the woods with Jonathan not far behind.

Just as the two boys were starting to feel they were safe, since they were at least a mile from the cemetery, they heard a gunshot.

They ran even faster as they knew someone must have been near.

The echo from the gunshot sounded as if it wasn't far away.

Standing behind the church, facing the cemetery and looking in the direction the boys had fled was an old man named Mr. Grub. He lived in between the Hill House and the church. His wrinkled hands gripped an old shotgun very tightly. He was wearing a red flannel jacket, stained with what appeared to be cat vomit. The hair he had left was white and looked as though he'd been struck by lightning once or twice.

- Taste -

"I'll teach you little bastards to wake my dogs again, next time I won't miss." Mr. Grub wiped the snot from his face with his sleeve.

"Earl, what the hell are you doing?" Mrs. Grub was standing outside on the front porch with her hands on her hips. Her husband looked back and waved his hand in disgust.

"Earl, get that goddamn gun back in here right now. Sheriff

Brady will be coming soon if you don't get your old ass moving."

Mrs. Grub shouted out loud enough for the entire town to hear. Earl Grub looked back toward his wife then once more toward the cemetery.

"I don't know what will be the death of me, those goddamn heathens or that bingo playing hag, lord knows I've been a sinner but come on now, at least have mercy on my old bones." He looked skyward as if waiting for a response.

"Earl!" his wife's crackly voice penetrated his skin once more.

"I'm coming, I'm coming," he said as he slowly walked back to his house. His wife stood in the doorway waiting. This was an everyday routine for the Grubs. Earl Grub would hear something and claim it woke up his dogs and run outside with his gun to check it out. Day in and day out this happened, and the funny thing was they didn't own any dogs.

Laughing uncontrollably across the street was a woman named Elmer Gene. She was in her eighties and was a retired schoolteacher. She found her amusement by day sitting on her front porch as well, but observing the actions of her neighbors.

"What are you laughing at Grandma?" A quiet voice spoke as the door opened. Elmer Gene turned around and smiled with delight toward her granddaughter.

- Taste -

"Oh nothing, Chrissie, just the townsfolk, that's all." The old woman sat back in her wooden rocking chair and stroked her longhaired feline, which was nestled snugly in her lap.

"Well, it's good to hear you laugh, Gram; I don't hear it as often as I should." Chrissie slowly walked past Elmer Gene and down the great stone steps toward the road.

"Where are you going, Chrissie?"

"I'm just going for a walk, Gram; I'll be back in a while", she said as innocently as she could.

"Well, don't be too long; you don't want to miss supper." "I won't," Chrissie yelled as she walked down the street. Chrissie had plans of her own. She knew the boys were playing football down the street because she could hear them from her bedroom. And most certainly one of those boys would be Jesse Hodge, a certain admirer of Chrissie's.

Walking through the streets that day was an event within itself.

The leaves were raging through the air due to the increase in wind. The colors from the leaves were beaming off one another almost as if they were individual light sources. It created an atmosphere for itself that day.

"All right, this is how we're going to do it," a scruffy fifteenyear-old said as his knuckles bled from attempting the most dramatic move there is in the game of football: the diving catch. Normally it's a move you try when you're running through the open field, where the ground becomes your partner. Not a move for the paved streets in the town of McDonough. But nobody would tell that to David Fearson. He'd just as soon dive on you while you're walking down the street with your parents and pound the crap out of you, just for the sake of doing it.

- Taste -

- Taste -

No reason whatsoever, and that's what made his brand of madness so devious. It would unleash with no predictability.

The teams were ready, it was fourth down. The six of them were beat up and battered. Every one of the boys was soaked head to toe. Pants were ripped, glasses were broken, and ankles were sprained. They stood facing each other and prepared for battle.

Standing next to David's right was Jimmy Phillips, a sixteen year-old who spent more time fishing than doing his school work, which was probably the reason he was still in seventh grade. Wasn't a scholar, but a hell of a fisherman he was. Standing at David's left was Eddie Mueller, a twenty four-year-old high school dropout who had been deemed the town's worst thug. Whenever there was any wrongdoing or vandalism, Ed was usually the first suspect. Ed and his family had moved up from Long Island seven years prior. I guess you can call this a transition stage for the Mueller's. Take a troubled kid from the city and throw him into a town full of misfits and loners, and you're bound for some mischief.

Directly facing David was Jesse Hodge, a nineteen-year-old whose daily activities typically consisted of stealing alcohol from his father's fridge, shooting cars with BB guns, spray painting road signs, and causing mayhem and distress among the older folk in town.

Standing to Jesse's left was Scott Martin, a twenty-year-old compulsive liar who still rode around on his bike. No matter what he was talking about, he would always throw in a lie about something. This grew annoying at times, but eventually people learned how to deal with it.

On Jesse's right was Billy Jacobs, a nerdy fifteen-year-old who broke his glasses once a week. His mother and father had died together in a car accident two years earlier.

- Taste -

Billy lived with his aunt and her several "patients" as he referred to them. Billy's aunt received a lot of money from the state to house certain mentally disabled individuals in her home. This made for many interesting visits to Billy's house, especially for Ed.

So here they were, the six lone guns on the street preparing for the last play. Jesse's team had the ball, but Brandon's team was three points ahead. The only chance for Jesse's team to win depended on this single play.

"Hut!" Jesse screamed as he moved back to avoid David's rushing lead. All of a sudden David's attention was on something else. Jesse noticed David was distracted by something and seized the moment. He ran past David and towards the grease spot in the road which stood for the touchdown marker. Meanwhile Scott Martin had succeeded in keeping Jimmy Phillips away from Jesse, but the same can't be said for Billy. Eddie had knocked Billy down instantly and was gunning for Jesse.

"Look what we have here," David roared toward a skinny kid approaching a mailbox near the street.

"Touchdown!" Jesse yelled as he threw the football down and celebrated his triumph. Billy and Scott raised their hands in the air to represent their win.

"Ah, who cares anyway, I'm going to get a beer. It's about that time." Eddie said to himself as he walked past Jesse and shook his hand.

"Wait a minute, Ed, what's David doing?" Ed turned around. David was walking toward Brandon McAllister with his hands up in the air. Brandon was opening up his mailbox and retrieving his mother's mail like she had asked him.

"Hey Gash, cut your self lately?" David shouted. Brandon's head was down and he quickly walked back to his house trying to ignore the insults.

"Yeah, go home you freak, go sit with your hog of a mother," David laughed as he stopped walking and stood near the mailbox with his chest puffed out.

Meanwhile Chrissie had snuck up behind Jesse and put her hands over his eyes.

"Guess who?" she said. Jesse quickly turned around and gave her a kiss, surprised to see her.

Ed waved his hand in the air and said,

"That kid asks for it, he never comes out of that house, and when he does he's asking for trouble." Jesse turned to Ed while he still held Chrissie in his arms.

"What does he do to ask for trouble? The kid might be a freak but he never bothers anyone, maybe he's just sick and tired of being fucked with so much, ya know."

Ed smirked with a sarcastic tone and said,

"Yeah, I guess. Well, until he stands up for himself, people are going to fuck with him, people like that." Ed pointed towards David.

When Brandon reached his front door he opened it and stopped halfway in and turned around, looking out toward David. His long dark hair was covering the right side of his face; he reached up and brushed it away.

"Go back in your house, you freak," and with those words Brandon shut the door and retreated to his room once again to look out his bedroom window and watch the seven of them walk down the road toward the center of town. The game must be over.

As the seven of them migrated down the street, Jesse hollered out to David. "You feel better now?" But he didn't wait for an answer. David's anger was clearly showing as he shouted out;

- Taste -

- Taste -

"What, you're telling me that freaky kid doesn't bug you out?" His hands were waving as he spoke. "I don't want to see him and that's that. He can stay in that cave of his and rot with his mother." Jesse just shook his head and ignored David's cruel remarks. Jesse might have been a wild kid, but at least he had morals.

It was now 5:22, almost time for dinner, almost six o'clock. The dreaded hour every teen longed to miss. No matter how dysfunctional the family was, it was always the same. Be home for dinner. That's what they said. Each and every one of those parents hoped just a little bit that their kid would show up, taking his place at the table. No matter how bad things were it was that one time to sit together as one and embrace the moment, not because you wanted to, but because you felt as though it was your obligation to fulfill this one request. No matter how much it hurt or what you thought afterward, you had to do it because nothing lasts forever.

A loud car could be heard in the distance. Its sound permeated the atmosphere as it grew closer. The seven young souls on foot began to disperse in their separate directions. Some headed home for dinner, others headed for destinations unknown to them at the time. Jesse and Ed continued to walk down the street. The two of them found themselves a spot on the wooden picnic table in front of the general store and took their places. This was a usual meeting place among the kids in this town. The General Store was the only store for thirty miles. Situated on one of the four corners, it provided a panoramic view of the town. One could see in four different directions from this table, thus enabling the boys to be right in the middle of whatever action this town offered.

Ed and Jesse's heads turned as a loud car flew in to the parking lot. It was an '86 tan Cavalier with a busted-out windshield.

- Taste -

Ultra white clear plastic and duct tape made its appearance anything but presentable. You couldn't help but laugh at this monstrosity when you saw it.

"Speak of the Devil," Jesse said as Ed stood up. A long-haired man jumped out of the driver seat and stood next to the door. He had an old red, white and blue bandanna wrapped around his head. It looked as though it had never been removed, dirty as it was. His name was Duck; he was Ed's older brother.

Ed quickly picked up a small rock and threw it toward the passenger window. After the rock bounced off, the door opened.

"What are you doing that for, Ed?" a very calm voice spoke. A middle-aged man leaned out of the car. Dirty as sin, long hair as well. He was wearing a double insulated flannel jacket, the type most wood-cutters use.

"What's up, one-eyed Curt?" Jesse hollered as he stood up and descended the porch steps. Curt had lost his right eye in a chainsaw accident with Duck a few years before. Apparently they were both drunk and cutting wood, as usual, when Curt tripped on a limb and fell into Duck's chainsaw. The problem was that it was running. It sliced the right side of this face and took his eye. Now he bears a long scar all the way down his face. He refuses to wear an eye patch, claims it's not natural.

"Oh, not much Jesse," Curt said as he looked toward Ed.

"You ready? Mom needs help moving that fridge," Duck said as he opened up a Milwaukee's Best Ice. The cheapest beer on the market, it was also the most potent.

"Yeah, I'm ready," Ed looked at Jesse. "Got to go home and do some shit, see you tomorrow."

"See ya tomorrow, Ed." Jesse waved as he started walking up the street. Ed jumped into the back seat and the car took off. Ed spoke up above the noise of the damaged muffler.

"Hey Duck, you seen Tom? He was supposed to stop by and drop some money off a while ago, I haven't seen him, figured he was with you somewhere." Ed looked out the window as Duck replied.

"He took off a few hours ago; went out with Nathan shooting somewhere. You know them guys; who knows what time they'll be back?" Duck said as he scratched his head.

"Tom's always got to take off when Mom needs help. It would be easier with all of us there but he always gets out of helping somehow." Ed's Long Island accent came out even stronger when he was angry. Tom was two years younger than Ed. Duck was the oldest brother.

"It's that new gun of his." Duck finished guzzling his beer and threw the can on the floor.

"It's always something with him, it's always something," Ed continued to stare out the window.

As Jesse started his walk home from the main intersection he couldn't help but look over to his left. The massive white pillars could still be seen through the overgrown wilderness. A stone wall surrounded the mansion. Certain spots were crumbling, but most of it was still intact. Jesse stopped and stood still for a moment, looking toward the house. He felt a slight chill sweep over his body as he looked up at the diamond-shaped window. He rubbed his hands together and started walking again. He looked back once more but kept walking, as he had a mile to go. Then all of a sudden a voice from above startled him.

- Taste -

"Hey Jesse, what are you doing?" Jesse flinched as the unexpected voice caught him by surprise. He looked around for a minute and then he noticed someone sitting in one of the tree branches on the edge of the stone wall.

"What are you doing up their, Vest?" Jesse hollered up. Jesse recognized the voice; it belonged to a strange individual indeed. It was John Vest, a man in his late twenties who suffered from what appeared to be multiple personality disorder. Most of the town's folk assumed he was only a nut. Nobody called him by his first name, it was always Vest. Vest struggled down off the branch and found himself dangling like a monkey in a tree. Jesse looked up and down the street to see if anyone was watching.

"Why don't you get down from their, Vest, hurry up before people start wondering what the hell you're doing."

"Oh I'm all right, Jesse," Vest let go and landed flat on his back, knocking the wind out of him as smashed to the ground below. Jesse quickly ran to his aid.

"Are you all right? Want me to call for help?" Jesse was trying not to laugh. Vest picked him self up off the ground and said, "Don't you worry 'bout a thing, Jesse. It's that Indian blood I got inside me. Keep's me strong no matter how high the fall." Vest was wearing an old brown leather jacket that he had picked up at a biker swap meet. His shoes were knee-high deer-skin moccasins he had made himself. Dangling from his neck was a bone necklace he constructed from picking up road kill.

"Yeah, that's right, you're an Indian this month," Jesse said as vest brushed himself off.

- Taste -

"What are you doing now, Jesse?" Vest was always looking for some company; he wasn't well liked at home.

"I'm headed home; have to work early in the morning with my dad."

"Oh" Vest said as he leaned up and pointed toward the branch he'd been sitting on.

"You see that, Jesse; from that spot I can see everything and no one even knows I'm there. Hell, you didn't even know I was above ya until I said something." Vest sounded proud in describing his new hiding spot.

"That's cool, Vest. Hey look, I've got to go. I'll see ya tomorrow." Jesse shook Vest's hand and took off.

"See ya later, Jesse," Vest sat down on the stone wall and took some chew out of his front pocket. As he filled his mouth with the stringy cancer, he turned around and gazed toward the mansion behind him. "Not even you knew I was hiding up there." Vest laughed as he turned around and faced the road. The diamond shaped window appeared to be fogging up from the inside, as if something was breathing close to the glass. As Jesse walked by Brandon McAllister's home he noticed the blinds in the side window suddenly shake and a figure retreating. As if Brandon could pass it off and act like he wasn't looking.

"Kid is a freak," Jesse said as he continued his dreaded walk home. Not far up the street from where he stood was the entrance to Lake Road. It was the only road in town with no street lights. It was a dirt road that led to higher ground and circled the lake above. It didn't connect to any other roads with the exception of one place. Slightly before Jesse's house was an old logging trail. It hasn't been used since the first settlers occupied the area. It was a seasonal road through over 50 miles of state land. It was referred to by the locals as Dear Creek Pass.

- Taste -

Chapter 5

The morning of October 15th was dark. It had been raining all night, so the roads were building up streams of their own along the edge. Thick mist and vapors were rising from the earth's floor. Orange salamanders scattered through the rocks and in and out of the tall grass as rodents trampled through the sponge-soaked earth. Violent gusts of wind were blowing odd shaped leaves in all directions. The trees swayed in the morning breeze, resembling a dance among giants.

A pack of coyotes hunting near the lake were in stealth mode. A scurrying rabbit hid in the brush while the snouts picked up on its trail. The rabbit was grayish in color, and it remained still as it watched a snout approach. The coyote was sniffing the ground as it picked up a scent. Then its head rose and its mouth opened just a little. The rabbit shook in a nervous twitch as it was scared to move, aware of what would happen if it was seen. Then just as the rabbit was losing all hope another rodent broke the silence and attracted the attention of the coyotes. Within a few moments the screams could be heard from the soon-to-be-eaten rodent. The rabbit slowly crept away in an attempt to escape but found itself in the jaws of another coyote.

- Taste -

- Taste -

As the pack continued to prowl, the leader grew cautious of the water's edge. The animals seemed to be aware of a change in the atmosphere. Primitive ways reign supreme in a natural setting.

"Wake up, you lazy bum. Wake up. I said, Wake up you lazy bum, wake up"! A foot-tall plastic novelty man spoke the words you hated to hear in the morning. Jesse tossed and turned as he opened his eyes and looked over toward his alarm clock. His father had bought the hokey thing at South of the Border and sent it home during one of his travels. It was not the type of thing you'd ever buy on your own.

The time read 7:40 on the tiny guitar held by the Mexican figure. As the toy continued to shake and move and sing, "Wake up, you lazy bum. Wake up!" Jesse sighed and said,

"I hate that thing." He laid back and looked up toward the ceiling. Posters of bands covered the ceiling and walls. He made himself get out of bed and venture into the living room. As he rubbed his eyes and yawned, he saw his father with his golf bag around his shoulder.

"Aren't we working today?" Jesse was confused.

"Well, it rained like hell all night so I don't think we can do the roof today," his dad replied as Jesse opened the fridge. Jesse pulled out a carton of orange juice and drank straight from the container.

Mr. Hodge quickly grabbed the drink out of Jesse's hand,

"What are you, sick? You don't do that. Get a glass like everyone else— I don't want your shit". Jesse tried not to laugh as he swallowed a mouthful.

"It's too wet outside to work on the roof but it's good enough to golf?" Jesse asked in a sarcastic tone. His father looked at him as he opened the kitchen door.

- Taste -

"What are you, my wife? I thought you'd be happy not to work today. Besides, the course will be closing down in a few days. See you later. There's five bucks on the table, near the mail." Mr. Hodge ran out the door and threw his clubs in the back of an '83 Ford F-150 and sped up the street.

"See ya," Jesse walked past the table and swiped the five. He noticed an unopened package addressed to his father lying on the table. It was from Jesse's grandfather, Claude Moore. Jesse grabbed a toaster strudel on his way to the shower. By the time he was finished it was almost 9:00. Jesse picked up the phone. He dialed Ed's number. The phone kept ringing and ringing.

"Come on, Ed, I know you're there," After no answer at Ed's house, Jesse called Scott Martin.

"Yeah," Scott said on the other line while he chewed on a piece of watermelon, spitting the seeds into a silver trash can.

"Hey, you've got to take me down to Ed's house".

"I'm not riding my bike all the way up your hill."

"No no," Jesse interrupted. "I'll meet you at your house, I'll walk down."

"OK, that's cool," Scott answered.

"Give me a few minutes."

"See ya in a few," Scott hung up the phone and lit up a cigarette. Jesse quickly ran out the door and headed for town. Jogging was usually the best way to travel on foot and make time.

Once Jesse reached Scott's house, which was across the street from Brandon McAllister's, they both jumped on Scott's orange Huffy. Scott was the driver and Jesse was on the handlebars. The bike was covered in bumper stickers. It even had a miniature headlight propped up on the front handle bars. There was also a homemade trailer he'd latch on when needed. He had this bike rigged up as if it were his sports car.

The boys rode through the main intersection and past the general store. They rode down the hill and headed for the bridge.

Ed lived a couple of miles away from the main intersection, over a bridge across the Genegantslet. As the boys coasted over the wooden bridge Jesse saw something out of the corner of his eye.

"Scott, stop for a second!" Jesse yelled back toward Scott. The bike came to a screeching halt. Jesse ran over to the edge and glared out toward the watery shore.

"What do you see?" Scott yelled as he opened a candy bar and threw the wrapper on the ground.

"Right there, see?" Jesse pointed toward an orange light near the water's edge.

"I see it now, what is it?"

"It looks like somebody walking around with some sort of flashing light." They were too far away to identify, but Jesse was able to make out a figure.

"Somebody must be looking for something."

"Yeah, I guess so."

As the boys rode up Ed's driveway, they noticed one police car and a black police truck parked between the house and the trailer. They knew the truck but wondered what was happening as the bike slowly came to a stop near an old dog house with the name Sweet Pea painted on the side.

"Watch out for that dog, Scott, he's not friendly." Just as the words left Jesse's mouth, the crazed black Labrador came rushing toward them, barking and snapping at Scott's feet.

- Taste -

- Taste -

Inside the house a tall, thick man glanced out the window to see what the commotion was about. He was wearing a green Carhartt jacket and an old Yankees hat.

"Looks like you have some company," Sheriff Brady said as he continued to pace the living room floor. The mood in the house was very still. Ed and his mother were both sitting on the couch while Duck was outside taking care of the animals. Sheriff Brady stood near the end of the couch and put his hand on Ed's mother's shoulder.. She was trying to hold back tears but her will wasn't strong enough. She was holding a framed picture in her hands.

"I'm sure Tom's all right, Mary, he's a bright enough boy. I'm sure there's a good reason why he hasn't come back yet. Probably got drunk somewhere and passed out. You know how those boys can be. I'm sure its nothing." He spoke in a calm voice as he patted Mary's back and tried to comfort her. Sheriff Brady then stood up and looked out the window once more.

"In any case, I've got my men out there right now tearing up every rock and looking through every bush this town has to offer. They'll show up." Brady couldn't help but feel bad for this poor woman. It didn't matter if her sons were hoodlums or not. She's still a mother and carries the motherly instinct.

Sheriff Brady made eye contact with Ed and waved him over to speak with him near the door. Ed took his arm off his mother's back and walked over. Sheriff Brady opened the door and turned around as he stood outside the house.

- Taste -

"You have my cell; call me whenever you feel the need, no matter what." Ed nodded his head as a single teardrop ran down his cheek. Brady reached over and gave Ed a good shake on the shoulders.

"Hey, we're going to find your brother. You have my word. Ed looked up and said,

"Look I'm really sorry for all those times I've caused you trouble. I know I can be a real pain sometimes." Sheriff Brady interrupted him;

"Ed, you and I have had our run-ins, but let's not worry about that right now. Let's find the boys."

Ed walked outside with Brady, Jesse and Scott stood cautiously near the cars trying not to intrude on whatever was happening. The Sheriff dug an old military-issue lighter out of his front pocket and lit a cigar, blowing the smoke up high as he breathed in the fumes of the tobacco. Brady caught sight of Jesse and Scott.

Immediately they both straightened up and stood tall.

"What's going on, Ed?" Jesse asked.

"Tom didn't come home last night. We didn't think anything of it until Brady showed up and told us that Nathan never made it home either. Nathan's parents called the police late last night. They said he was with Tom since early yesterday afternoon." Ed made a gasping sound in his throat and spit out an awful looking chunk of lung, yellowish in color.

'You boys haven't seen Tom or Nathan anywhere, have you?" the sheriff asked. Jesse and Scott both quickly responded.

"I haven't seen either one for at least a few days now." Scott replied.

"I saw Tom's car parked at the store yesterday," Jesse said. This triggered the Sheriff's attention a bit and he took the cigar out of his mouth.

"What time did you see him?" Jesse had to think back.

- Taste -

"It was early afternoon, had to've been close to 2:00. It was before you showed up in town, Ed". Jesse looked over in Ed's direction. The Sheriff pulled a small pad of paper out of his pocket and scribbled down a few notes.

"All right, you boys let me know the minute you know something, you hear?"

"Yes sir," Ed walked past Jesse and Scott and leaned toward

Brady. Brady was now sitting in his truck with the engine running.

"As soon as I have some news you'll be the first to hear. Same goes for you. Let me know the minute he shows up so I can race over here and give him hell for putting us all through this." He looked for a response from Ed but understood why it didn't come through.

"Talk to you soon," Ed smacked the door and walked away in the direction of his friends. Brady pulled out of the driveway and immediately got on his radio.

"Jim, where are you at?" he asked his deputy, whose car was still parked in Ed's driveway. A scrambled transmission came through the radio.

"I'm a little ways past the bridge now, haven't found nothing yet." Ed's house was situated on the edge of the Genegantslet stream. Brady had sent his deputy behind the house near the water's edge with the orders to work his way down the stream.

"Keep going for now. I'm headed uptown. I'll call you in a while." Brady puffed on his cigar and headed for the one destination he hoped would provide some answers. He was driving to the general store.

Jesse wasn't quite sure how to take this encounter, let alone how to approach Ed afterward. What would he say? He didn't think mentioning how he had seen Vest in a tree or how he had managed to smuggle some more beer from his father's fridge would be the right thing to do, given the circumstances. What now?

Scott's cigarette hung from his lips as though it were glued on as he scrubbed fresh mud from his bike with his T shirt.

"So yeah, that's what's going on today. Always something 'round here." Ed quickly wiped his face and grew tense as he walked back towards the house. Jesse followed.

Inside the house, Ed's mother was still sitting on the couch. The framed picture she had held was now shattered on the wooden floor at her feet. Ed ran up the stairs and Jesse stood near the door, lingering neither outside nor inside of the house. He couldn't help but look at Ed's mother as she sat motionless, still, her eyes open. The tears were no longer coming forth. Jesse shivered as he stepped outside and out of range for her to see him.

Duck suddenly appeared, carrying a five gallon bucket in each hand. His blue jeans were black from wear and his saggy flesh was ridden with grass and dirt.

"How the hell can you walk around with no shirt, Duck. It's cold."

"Sleep in this place long enough and you'll be fucked up, too." Duck walked past Jesse and headed into the house. Jesse heard some shouting and immediately made his way over to Scott, who was a good distance away. It seemed the farther away you were from something the better you'd feel.

"Talk about showing up at the wrong time."

"Yeah," Scott was now re-wiring the headlight.

"What are you doing?"

"A few modifications on this light and it will be way more powerful." Scott coughed as he stood up and stretched.

- Taste -

- Taste -

"That's what you're thinking about right now? What about Tom and Nathan?" Jesse looked away in disgust.

"Well, if I hitch the trailer on to the bike I can transport a car battery in the trailer. Then I can wire the battery to the light and it should be more powerful."

"What about the size of the headlight, won't it need to be bigger since you have more power running to it?" Scott was puzzled for a minute as he looked at Jesse.

"You know, I never thought about that." Scott said as he wiped his face and lit another cigarette.

"Here comes Ed. I wonder what he's going to do." Jesse looked toward the house after Scott spoke.

"Hey, what are you guys gonna do?" Ed asked as he got closer. Both of them looked at one another and then Jesse said, "Nothing, we just came down to see what's up with you." Ed was now standing next to them.

"Well, stick around for a few minutes and I'll take off with you guys."

"You're not going to stay here?" Scott asked.

"And do what, sit around and mope? Tom's got mom all worked up for nothing, and to tell you the truth, I don't really want to be here when he does decide to show up. No, I've gotta get out of here." Ed's face was stern and bitter looking. This is what Ed needed. He spent a lot of time on the streets and although the streets in this town were totally different than what he was used to, it was where Ed needed to be.

"I'll have Duck give us a ride as soon as he gets cleaned up. You can throw the bike in the trunk if you want a ride, Scott." Scott tried not to show his nervous tension about having his bike in the trunk of a car. It might get scratched.

- Taste -

"I've got to go back in the house for a minute, I'll be back," Ed said.

"Ok," Jesse replied. Scott was rubbing his hands together and blowing on them in an attempt to keep warm.

"Sure is getting cold, isn't it? The goddamn wind is something fierce."

"It's October, almost winter. The days are getting shorter." Jesse looked down at his feet. His black boots were surrounded by a red puddle.

"What the hell?" Scott looked over as Jesse backed up.

"What's the matter?" Scott's eyes drifted down towards the ground and followed the red trail to the source some twenty feet away. Lying in the dirt was Sweet Pea. As the boys approached the dog, its mouth hung open. Its eyes were colorless, sunken in to the inner depths of the skull.

"What happened to it?" Scott whispered. They both knelt down and looked the dog over. The origin of blood had come from the dog's mouth. Jesse stared at the stream of blood and then at the dog. The blood had traveled over twenty feet to reach Jesse and Scott.

"How did the blood travel that far?" Jesse looked at Scott as they both stared at one another for what felt like an eternity.

Chapter 6

"Look at that wind blowing; it's getting stronger by the day." Mr. Anderson said to his wife as she worked on her daily crossword puzzle. Mr. Anderson stood behind the cash register and gazed out the window of the general store.

"It's damn near blowing the metal off the roof next door. You see that, Irene?"

"Yes dear, that's nice," she said as she continued to work on the puzzle. She was engrossed in her own thought, not knowing what her husband had even said. He glared at her.

"You don't even know what I just said," he scowled. Irene suddenly awoke from her self-induced daze.

"What, dear?" she said as her husband turned around and looked out the window once more.

"Forget it." The veins in his arms were bright blue and were sticking out for all to see. A tattoo was half hidden beneath the white collared shirt he wore. Located on his right forearm was a faded cross. An eagle stood behind, its claws grasping the cross. A vehicle pulled hurriedly into the vacant parking lot.

- Taste -

"Sheriff's here. Must be something going on for Brady to drive all the way up from Oxford."

"It's probably the Grubs down the street, that or those damn Long Island nuisances."

As the door opened, a bell hung from above jingled ever so slightly. The bell's purpose was to notify the owners of someone's presence inside the store, although most of the time it didn't work. The wooden floor was uneven in spots due to the winter heaving and shifting of the ground below. It seemed every year the bottom of the door would scrub across the floor worse and worse.

Brady greeted the owners and poured himself a cup of coffee. After a few minutes of chat Brady informed them of the current situation. He learned that Tom had bought a sandwich and a few boxes of twenty gauge shells. As to where he was headed, one could only guess. Brady walked through the aisles of the store. An undisturbed layer of dust covered most shelves. His footsteps rattled through the stone basement below. Echoing off the walls.

"How do you guys keep this place going?" he asked as he picked up an old stack of postcards and shuffled through them.

"I've been here nearly twenty years now," Mr. Anderson coughed. "And I have a feeling this place is going to pick up in more ways that one." His head nodded as he spoke, as if to remind himself of his own goals and expectations.

"I sure hope so," Brady said as he tipped his hat toward Mrs. Anderson and opened the front door.

"Oh, I don't want to take these," Brady put the stack of postcards on the counter. On the top of the pile was a photograph of a horse and carriage

- Taste -

- Taste -

driving through the center of town. Behind the carriage the Hill House can be seen, surrounded by massive pine trees.

"You folks have a nice day." As he prepared to shut the door, Mrs. Anderson spoke up.

"Sheriff Brady. Why is it you came all the way up here from New York in the first place? Most folks that live around here were either born here or they can't get out of here. It's quite irregular that someone would relocate here just for the sake of doing so." Brady bit his lips and thought to himself for a moment. Goddamn small townspeople think they know everything, and what they don't they're sure to make up.

"I moved to Oxford because they were in need of a Sheriff. Not because I was running away from anything." Mr. Anderson and his wife both looked up.

"I didn't say anything about you." Brady quickly interrupted.

"Anyhow, I enjoy the seclusion this area offers to the soul. You folks have a nice day." The door was shut and the store's owners looked at one another with bewildered expressions.

Brady sighed absent-mindedly and lit his cigar once again as he stood on the front porch looking across the street where stray dogs had caught a chicken and were fighting over it. Elmer Gene was known as the chicken lady by the townspeople. She had hundreds of chickens, but she didn't provide any fencing for them. They ran through the town unattended and wild. This was another unique trait of McDonough. Not only were there stray dogs running as a pack, hundreds of chickens made the streets and neighboring lawns their natural living atmosphere, shitting on everything and causing major disturbance among certain townsfolk. Brady pulled his cell phone out of his front pocket and dialed.

- Taste -

"Goddamn shit." He turned the phone off after realizing there was no signal.

"This has got to be the last place left where a cell phone doesn't work."

"One of 'em." The voice startled Brady.

"What the hell are you doing, Vest, creeping around like that?" Vest emerged from the side of the building.

"You know why those technical phones like that you're carrying won't work around here, don't you?"

"Enlighten me, Vest, enlighten me." Brady stood near the driver's door of his truck.

The government's got you all bugged up, yep." His voice was hoarse from spending so much time outdoors and often he would pause between thoughts.

"Every time you people use those things, they know where you are. All they have to do is look in their computers and wham!

They've got ya." He punched his hands together.

"That's certainly interesting, Vest." Brady smiled as he opened the door and got into his truck.

"I'm serious, Sheriff. They know. Why is it you think I hang around here? Cause there's no satellites in these parts. Only place left where they can't find ya." A call came over the radio. Brady answered into the microphone that was attached to the door.

"Yeah, go ahead, Jim." He took a sip from his coffee.

"Meet me at the bridge right now. I'm not going any further, I'm headed back now." Vest's face picked right up as Brady quickly tried to intervene.

"Uh yeah, that sounds like a plan." Brady looked at Vest and knew that he had heard the transmission.

"He sounded kind of nervous." Vest paused for a second and took a breath.

"Over that radio I mean." Vest had no need to say anything else. He got his point across plainly enough. Could have kept it to himself, but that wasn't Vest.

"Nice talking to you, John." Brady threw it into reverse and backed up aggressively, then took off down the hill.

As Duck's car pulled itself up the hill and the general store came in sight, the four inside watched Brady pass by. Not a single person in the car spoke. But all experienced the same train of thought. Each of them wondered where Tom and Nathan were.

Vest had walked across the street and was standing on the corner of the Hill estate when Duck pulled into the store's parking lot.

"I wonder what's going on?" Vest said as he watched Duck's car unload three passengers and a bike and then take off down the hill once again.

"Who gives a sailing shit what you think, whiny little punk. Yeah that's it, keep talking. You know you hear me. Can't escape me." Vest was startled and he spun around looking for the source of these accusations.

"What's the matter, can't you find me?" Vest grabbed his head and squeezed.

Ed just so happened to catch Vest having his fit across the road and yelled out.

"Don't worry about it, Vest, it's all in your head." He turned and faced Jesse.

"He's a fucking maniac. Look at him. Admire this rare quality 'cause no town's got anything as fucked up as Vest. Motherfucker could have books written about him and no one would buy them 'cause it's too fucked up to see. First he's a priest and then he's a Nazi. Motherfucker walks around town in a Nazi uniform in the dead of winter. And I mean original handcrafted swastika wearing vintage bootleg whatever the hell you want to call it uniform shit!"

It was good to see Ed behave more like his old self again. Even in times as chaotic as these, people need to escape one reality and embrace another. Degrading one's actions can be self-healing in more ways than one.

Ed pulled the zipper and opened up his backpack as he walked across the street and took out two cans of beer.

"I think you need one of these just as much as I do, maybe even more." Ed handed Vest a beer and sat on the stone wall that circled the Hill estate. They cracked 'em open and Vest held the can close to his ear and listened as it popped and sizzled inside. Ed looked at him.

"What are you doing?" "Listening," Vest said.

"Listening to what?"

"Whatever they tell me." Vest turned his head and looked toward the Hill House.

"OK, that's enough of that shit; you either slam it in one shot or drink it like a bitch." Ed pounded his beer. So did Vest.

Branches from enormous pine trees draped over the stone wall in most spots. It could be raining hard as hell and you wouldn't get wet. It acted as a roof or a type of shelter from the elements above. You could sit on the stone wall and see everything around you but no one would be able to see you within the thick covering of pine.

This aspect provided the best hiding spots imaginable.

Not to mention a sleeping place for the chickens. Chicken smashing became a demented sport for these young minds in town. Often they would designate an individual who would have to climb the tree and rip the chickens down so they could violently be smashed to pieces by the bats, two by fours, rakes, shovels, or whatever they could get their hands on at the time. Oh, you didn't know? Chickens sleep in trees at night.

"What a messed-up day." Jesse looked at Scott as they stood in the parking lot of the store.

"You're telling me?" Scott said. "I can't even register what the fuck's going on." Scott looked at Jesse and spoke again.

"I can't get that dog out of my mind. Its mouth looked so wide, so open." Scott lit another cigarette. Jesse noticed Scott's hands were shaking slightly as he fumbled with his lighter.

"It must have had a heart attack or something. I mean we were outside the whole time and we didn't hear anything. It didn't make a noise or anything."

"Yeah, but Jesse, did you see Duck just throw the dog into one of his buckets like it was a piece of trash or something? It didn't even bother him. The dog's bloody mouth was draped over the side of the bucket and Duck didn't even pay attention. It's like nobody wanted to admit that something unnatural happened. Blood doesn't just travel along the ground and end up near your fucking feet. It's like it wanted to be near us. It knew we were there."

Jesse smirked and said, "Oh come on now, Scott, you're acting like Vest now. It wanted to be near us. What the hell." Jesse started to walk across the street.

"You coming, Scott?" Scott's eyes looked watery and his nose was starting to run.

"I don't know, Jesse. I don't know."

- Taste -

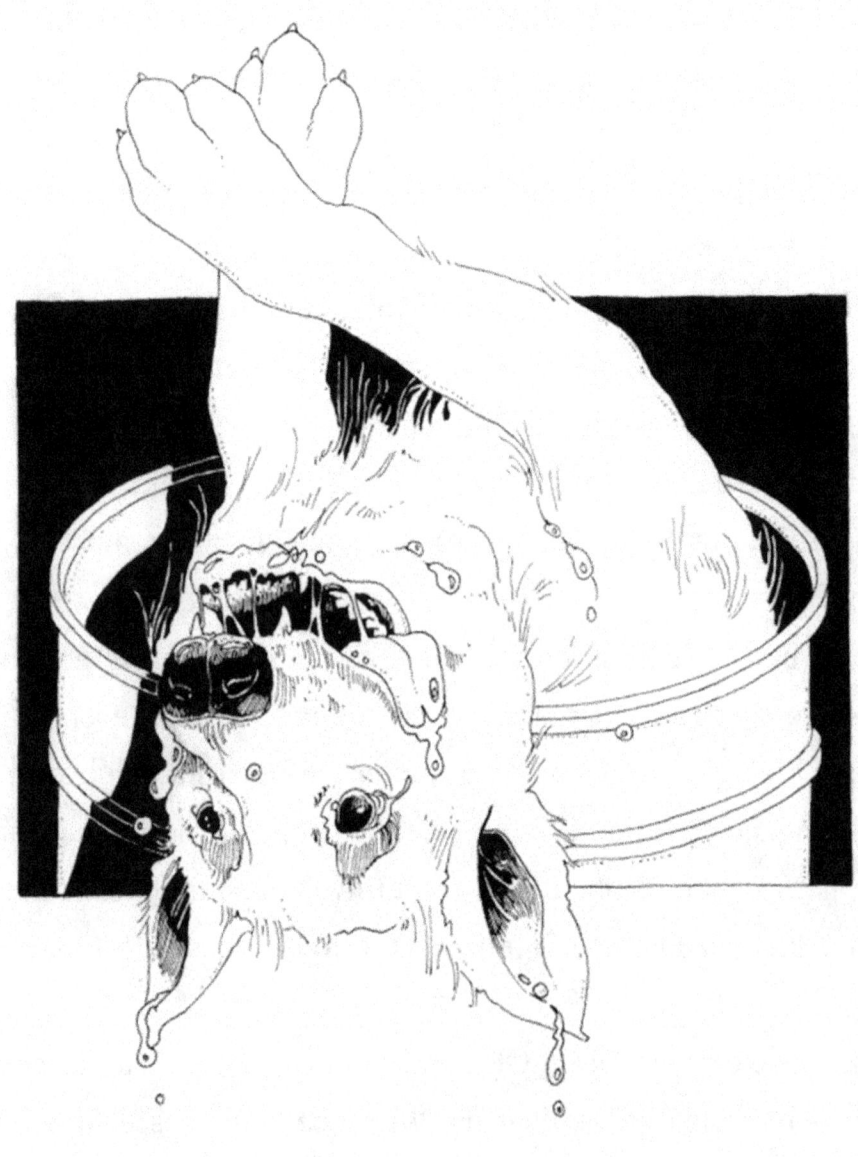

- Taste -

Meanwhile, Brady parked his truck on the side of the road near the bridge and was already over the guard rails. He was standing on the edge of the stream when he tried to reach Jim on the radio.

"Jim, where are you, what's going on?" He waited for a moment. There was no answer. The flowing water made it almost impossible to hear anything except that of flowing water. He tried once more.

"Jim, where are you?" Still no answer. Brady looked at his portable radio to make sure that it was working properly. The switch was turned on and the volume was all the way up. Then he noticed the red power light wasn't on. He shook the radio and banged it across his hands.

"Goddamn thing." He threw it on the ground and raced up to the truck. He opened the door and grabbed the radio inside and tried again.

"Jim, where are…" he stopped immediately, puzzled. He reached over and turned the switch on and off and there was no power running to that one, either. He started the engine and hoped it would provide an answer. It didn't. The radio inside the truck was not working.

"What the hell?" Brady stepped back and rubbed his face and thought for a minute.

"Brady," Jim's voice traveled along side the howling wind.

"Jim, where the hell are you?" Brady hollered as he made his way over the rusty guard rails and headed for the stream's edge.

Jim was frantically running toward Brady as he stood on the water's edge below the bridge.

"What's the matter, Jim?" Brady asked. He didn't know what to expect. Had Jim found something? Was it the boys? What was it? Ideas bombarded Brady's mind as Jim approached.

- Taste -

"Jesus Christ, Jim you're soaking wet." Jim's body was drenched. He looked as though he had jumped into a swimming pool with all of his clothes on.

"What happened?" Brady said again.

Jim had now reached Brady and was sitting on the ground

trying to catch his breath. As Jim's lungs heaved, he looked up toward Brady.

"I don't know what happened. I was walking down the stream like you said and out of nowhere something jumped out at me."

"Something as in…"

"I don't know what, but I'm not going back down there." Jim was shivering.

"An animal or what?" Brady said.

"It moved so fast I couldn't tell what it was. I was walking on that side." Jim pointed to the left side of the stream.

"All of a sudden I felt like something was watching me." Brady's eyes started to wander as he listened to Jim, scanning the area for whatever may be present.

"I know it's easy to get all worked up, especially when we're working on a situation like this. But I'm telling you, I knew something was there. I felt it. That's when I called you."

"You radioed me before you saw it?"

"Hell yeah, I wasn't going any further. I felt it inside the pit of my stomach. Something was wrong and I wasn't about to find out what."

"We've got to get you dry. You'll get ill in this wicked cold." Brady helped Jim get to his feet and the two of them stood still and looked downstream. The wind was making waves along the surface of the water.

Brady took his coat off and threw it over Jim, who was shivering violently; his fingertips were starting to turn blue.

"Let's go for now," Brady said as he tried to nudge Jim forward.

"I thought it was behind me when I first felt its presence. I was sure of it. But when it jumped out it was in front of me. Not behind." Jim looked at Brady.

"I didn't imagine it. That I know. But what it was I have no idea. It didn't resemble anything I've ever seen before. Its body was so limber, so long." Both men looked at one another and then at the stream.

The rocks were glistening from beneath the water as the sun penetrated. Although clouds were on the horizon, the sun managed to squeak by and shine its powerful essence in certain areas.

"Let's go," Brady repeated as he pushed Jim forward. Looking down the stream Brady noticed how the shrubbery and trees on the stream's edge seemed to lean in. Its effect was so overwhelming it appeared to block out the sky from above. A tunnel is what the stream resembled as Brady glared back once more and made his way up to the road.

Brady grabbed a duffel bag out of the back of the truck and handed it to Jim.

"There's a change of clothes in there, might be a little big but it'll do."

"Thanks," Jim said as he hopped into the cab of the truck and proceeded to get undressed. Brady shut the back hatch and walked over to the driver door. He felt the left side of his jacket and realized what he had left behind.

"Damn." He opened up the driver's door and grabbed the microphone inside. He clicked on the side button and listened to the sound waves which made a noise when you were about to make a call.

"It's working." He looked over towards Jim.

- Taste -

"Why wouldn't it be?" Jim said.

"When I first got down here, the radio…" He paused and looked down toward the stream.

"What about the radio?"

"I left my portable down near the water. I'll be right back." Brady slammed the door. The windows of the truck were starting to frost over.

"Hey, wait a minute." Brady stopped and turned around as Jim hollered out the passenger window.

"Be careful."

"I always am." Brady smiled as he turned around and climbed over the rusty guard rails for the fifth time. Hidden within the massive palm of his right hand was a 45.

He slowly walked down the hill to the water's edge. He was aware of everything that could be seen with the naked eye: multicolored leaves falling from gray branches above; crayfish scurried from the water's edge and concealed themselves among the many rocks under the water; bright green algae covering the rocks glowed as though it were fluorescent.

Brady stoopped and picked up the radio he had thrown down earlier. The red light was on. He turned it on and off and then spoke into it.

"Jim, you hear me?" He moved it away from his mouth and turned toward the bridge. The gusts of wind created a loud piercing sound as it traveled above the water and below the wooden bridge. The metal bridge supports echoed as the wind ricocheted off of them.

"Yeah, I hear you; you see something?" Jim's voice was eager with anticipation. He probably hoped Brady had seen something so that way Jim wasn't alone in the world of the loonies.

"No, just checking the radio." Brady stood up and prepared to walk back to the road until something in the water caught his attention. The reflection from the sun was beaming off something under the water. Brady moved closer to get a better look.

It appeared as though a silvery substance remained on the stream's floor. Brady pulled his sleeve up and dipped his arm into the icy water. Attempting to grab whatever it was underneath, goose bumps instantly covered his arm.

As he raised his arm out of the water he now realized what he had found. Close to five inches in length and bearing no written name on the handle. He quickly ran up to the road and jumped into the truck which was now running and quite warm inside. He threw the object on the front dash and opened up a bottle of aspirin and slammed three of them with his cold coffee.

"Everything all right?", Jim asked as Brady sat back and looked out the window toward the stream. Jim looked at the object Brady had thrown on the dash. Yellow and blue stripes ran down the handle.

"Where'd you get that?" Jim asked. Without facing Jim, still looking out the window, with his right hand on his cheek, Brady spoke.

"It's just a screwdriver Jim, just a screwdriver."

- Taste -

www.ingramcontent.com/pod-product-compliance
Lightning Source LLC
LaVergne TN
LVHW081453060526
838201LV00050BA/1786